This handwriting workbook has three comprehensive and engaging sections.

Section 1: Learning and Writing the Alphabet

In this fun-filled and engaging section, let your child trace the big dotted letters first and then write down the letters in the lined space. The fun part is they get to color 26 cool Pokemon. coloring pages. So, get the crayons ready!

Section 2: Writing Words

In this section, let your child learn some simple words and then some complex words. They can trace the words first and then write the words in the blank lined space.

Section 3: Write Full Sentences

This final section involves teaching your child how to write simple sentences. Did anyone say it was boring? These sentences are hilarious jokes and riddles! Have fun!

Section I: Learning and Writing the Alphabet

Trace the big dotted letters first, then write down the letters in the lined space. Also, color those 26 Pokemon

The letter A.
A is for Airplane

ARTICUNO

Practice Page

Practice Page

The letter B
B is for Bee

BAYLEEF

Practice Page

Practice Page

The letter C
C is for Cow

CHARIZARD

Practice Page

Practice Page

The letter D
D is for Dog

DRAGONITE

Practice Page

Practice Page

The letter E
E is for Egg

EEVEE

Practice Page

Practice Page

The letter F
F is for Fish

FOONGUS

Practice Page

Practice Page

The letter G
G is for Girl

GENGAR

Practice Page

Practice Page

The letter H
H is for Honey

HAPPINY

Practice Page

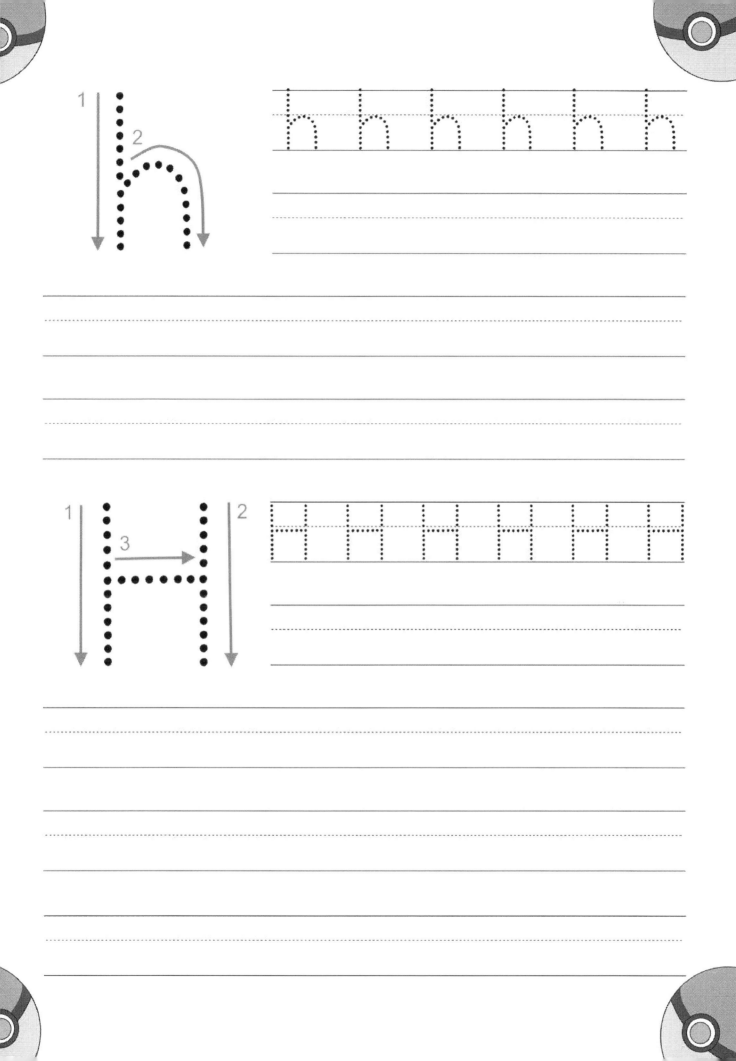

Practice Page

The letter I
I is for Ink

INKAY

Practice Page

Practice Page

The letter J
J is for Jug

JIGGLYPUFF

Practice Page

Practice Page

The letter K
K is for Key

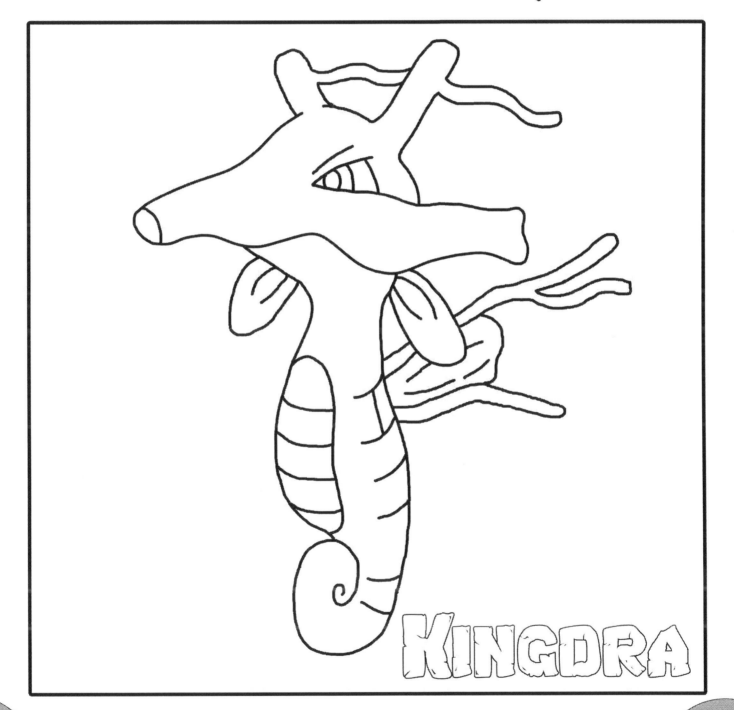

KINGDRA

Practice Page

Practice Page

The letter L
L is for Lamp

Practice Page

Practice Page

The letter M
M is for Moon

MUDKIP

Practice Page

Practice Page

The letter N
N is for Nurse

NATU

Practice Page

Practice Page

The letter O
O is for Orange

OMANYTE

Practice Page

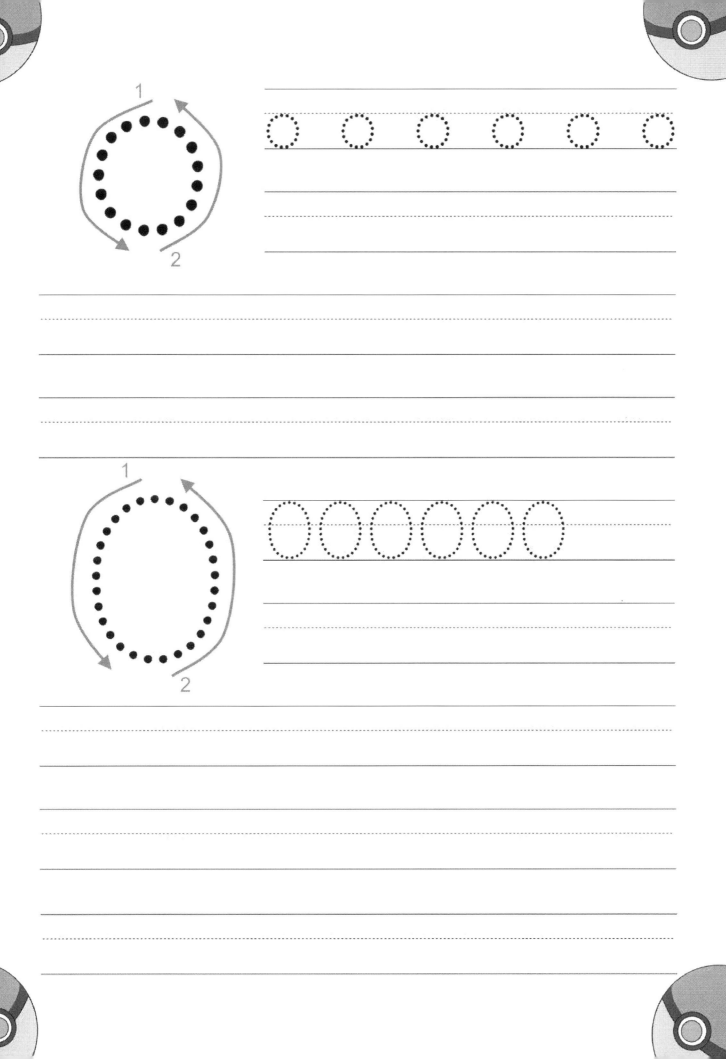

Practice Page

The letter P
P is for Pen

Practice Page

Practice Page

The letter Q
Q is for Queen

QWILFISH

Practice Page

Practice Page

The letter R
R is for Rabbit

ROWLET

Practice Page

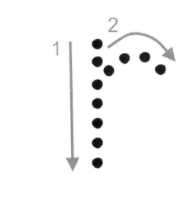

r r r r r r

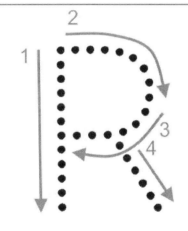

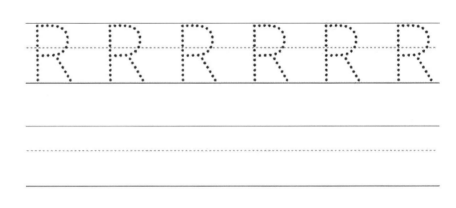

Practice Page

The letter S
S is for Ship

SQUIRTLE

Practice Page

Practice Page

The letter T
T is for Train

TEPIG

Practice Page

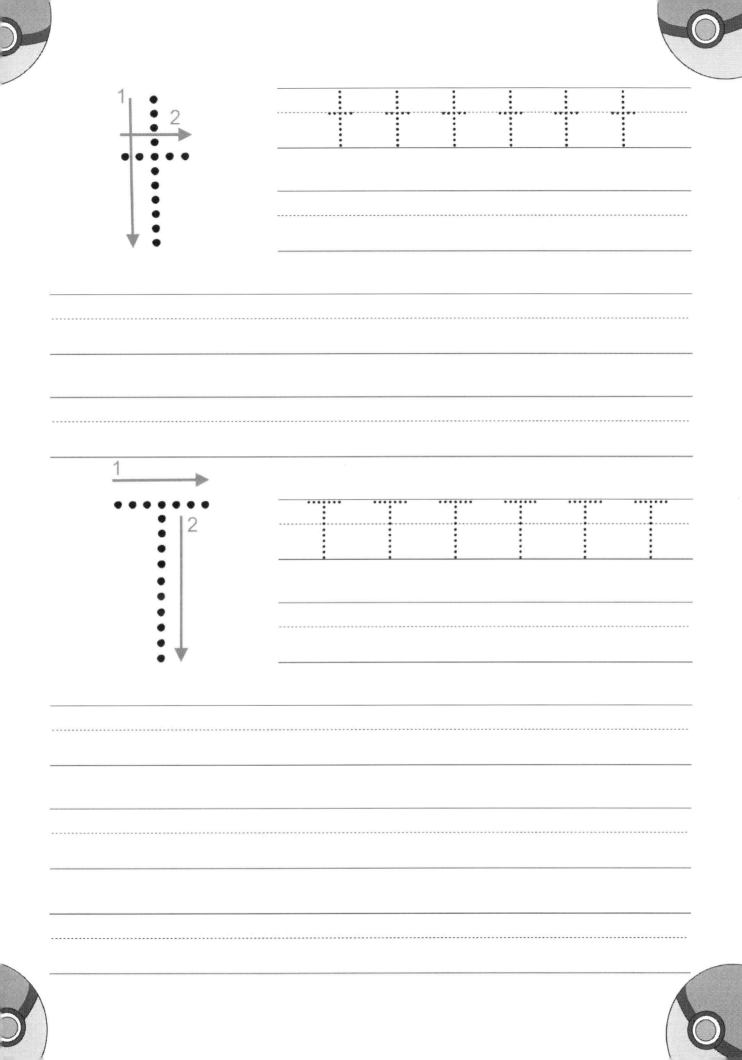

Practice Page

The letter U
U is for Umbrella

UMBREON

Practice Page

Practice Page

The letter V
V is for Vet

VICTINI

Practice Page

Practice Page

The letter W
W is for Window

WEEPINBELL

Practice Page

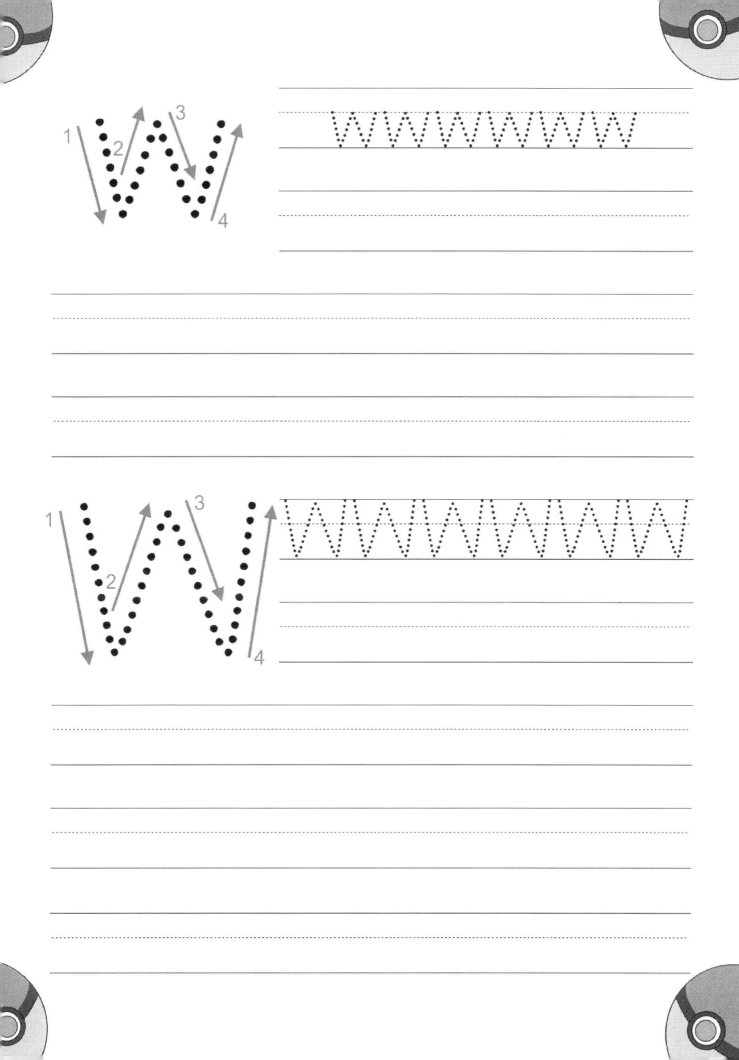

Practice Page

The letter X
X is for X-ray

XATU

Practice Page

Practice Page

The letter Y
Y is for Yak

YAMASK

Practice Page

Practice Page

The letter Z
Z is for Zig Zag

Practice Page

Section 2: Writing words

Use the knowledge from the previous section to write down some words. Trace the dotted words first, then write down the words in the lined space.

day day day day

bed bed bed bed

can can can can

had had had had

ten ten ten ten ten

home home home

not not not not

out out out out

ride ride ride ride

fish fish fish fish

down down down

when when when

snow snow snow

moon moon moon

next next next next

look look look look

very very very very

your your your

open open open

page page page

grass grass grass

help help help

make make make

time time time

living living living

eating eating

walking walking

people people

called called

asked asked

crying crying

quick quick quick

visited visited

which which which

would would would

yellow yellow

almost almost

instead instead

hospital hospital

where where

please please

under under

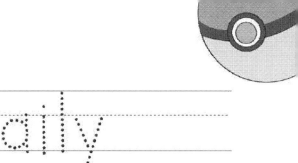

daily daily daily

mainly mainly

usually usually

could could could

every every every

know know know

Section 3: Writing Full Sentences

Use the knowledge from previous sections to make some sentences. Trace and then write yourself. Rejoice! These are jokes and riddles!!

Why did the girl
bury her flashlight?

Because the batteries
died

Which day do fish

hate?

Fryday

What goes to bed
with it's shoes on?

A horse

What do you call a
cow in a tornado?

A milkshake

What has a ring, but

no finger?

A telephone

What fish only

swims at night?

A starfish

Where is the cow
going for holiday?

Moo York

What is a ghost's
favorite fruit?

boo-berries

How do rabbits

travel?

By hare plane

What do cats call

Santa Clause?

Santa paws

What is tornado's favorite game?

Twister

What is at the end
of everything?

The letter G

Which bank has

no money?

Riverbank

Why was the math book sad?

It had too many problems

What disease can fly?

The flu

What do you give
a lemon in distress?

Lemonade

Can February March?

No, but April May

What has four
wheels and flies?

A garbage truck

What do you call
a snail on a ship?

A snailor

What 8-letter word
has one letter in it?

Envelope

Made in the USA
San Bernardino, CA
01 November 2019